has to do for her horse. It's hard to keep them all straight.

# a COWGIRL
# and her HORSE

By Jean Ekman Adams

**Rio Chico**
Books for Children

Rio Chico, an imprint of Rio Nuevo Publishers®
P. O. Box 5250, Tucson, AZ 85703-0250
(520) 623-9558, www.rionuevo.com

Editorial: Theresa Howell
Book design: David Jenney

Printed in China.

6   5   4   3                    13   14   15   16

Library of Congress Cataloging-in-Publication Data

Adams, Jean Ekman, 1942-
  A cowgirl and her horse / Jean Ekman Adams.
      p. cm.
  Summary: A young cowgirl demonstrates her unique way of caring
for her horse, from feeding him hay sandwiches to helping him pick
out new shoes.
  ISBN-13: 978-1-933855-71-4 (hardcover : alk. paper)
  ISBN-10: 1-933855-71-1 (hardcover : alk. paper)
  [1. Cowgirls—Fiction. 2. Horses—Fiction. 3. Human-animal
relationships.]  I. Title.
  PZ7.A2163Cow 2011
  [E]—dc23
                          2011018281

For
Annie, April, and Bill,
who found each other

There are so many things a cowgirl has to do for her horse.
It's hard to keep them all straight.

First, she has to feed him proper horse food.

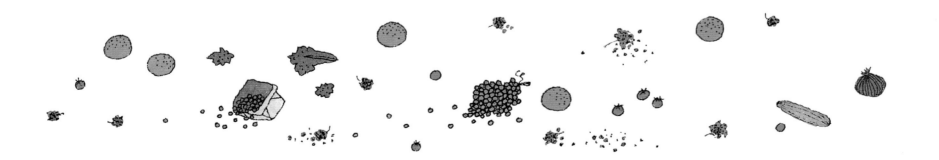

She must fix up a nice place for him to sleep.

She has to keep him warm on cold wet nights,

And she has to cool him off when it sizzles.

She must let him sniff the saddle before he puts it on,

And when he rounds up his
friends, she always helps.

Every two months, she has to help him pick out new shoes.

She can't forget his birthday,

And she must protect him from rattlesnakes.

She has to make sure he drinks enough water,

And she has to help him write letters home to his mother.

On his day off,
she has to take him for a ride,

And when they stop for lunch,

She has to order for him.

She has to wash his socks,

Comb his hair,

Clean his room,

And cut up lots of apples and carrots.

It is a lot of work.

But, he takes her up the mountain,

Down the trail,

And over the rainbow.

Because she is his cowgirl,
And he is her horse.